FOR TED AND THE THURSDAY TROUPE.
—M.M.

FOR MY BROTHER NICK, WITH LOVE AND THANKS.
—I.L.

# MIREILLE MESSIER
# AND IRENE LUXBACHER

# TREASURE

ORCA BOOK PUBLISHERS

Let's go find a treasure.

Okay!

How will we know when we've found a treasure?

Well, a treasure is shiny and mysterious and precious.
And the *best* treasures are always hidden.

Is this a treasure?

No. It's not shiny enough.

Is this a treasure?

No. Not mysterious enough.

How about this?

No. Not precious enough.

Humph! Finding a treasure is hard...

**Finding a treasure is fun!**

Are you sure there is a treasure?

**Not a bit!**

Will you share the treasure with me if we find it?

**As long as you help me carry it.**

Okay. I have pockets. But what if the treasure is too heavy?

**I have pockets too.**

The treasure is hidden too well!

We might be getting close.

The treasure is hidden too far away! I give up.

Just a little bit farther.

**I knew it!
I've found a treasure!**

Is it shiny?

**Yes!**

Is it mysterious?

**Oh yes!**

Is it precious?

**Yes!**

Will it fit in my pocket?

**No way!**

Let me see!

Wow! That's our treasure?

Yes! Some treasures are too big for pockets.

Goodbye, treasure.

**Cataloguing in Publication information available from Library and Archives Canada**

Issued in print and electronic formats.
ISBN 9781459817340 (hardcover) | ISBN 9781459817357 (pdf)
| ISBN 9781459817364 (epub)

Library of Congress Control Number: 2019934060
Simultaneously published in Canada and the United States in 2019

Also available as *Trésor*, a French-language picture book (ISBN 9781459823273)

**Summary**: In this gorgeously illustrated picture book, a brother and sister explore their surroundings, looking for treasure.

*Orca Book Publishers is committed to reducing the consumption of nonrenewable resources in the making of our books.
We make every effort to use materials that support a sustainable future.*

Orca Book Publishers gratefully acknowledges the support for its publishing programs provided by
the following agencies: the Government of Canada, the Canada Council for the Arts and
the Province of British Columbia through the BC Arts Council and the Book Publishing Tax Credit.

Artwork hand rendered on paper using graphite, watercolors, acrylic paints, soft pencil crayons and found papers.
It was digitally documented, further composed and printed using archival-quality inks and papers.

Cover and interior artwork by Irene Luxbacher
Edited by Liz Kemp
Design by Rachel Page

ORCA BOOK PUBLISHERS
orcabook.com

Printed and bound in China.

22 21 20 19 • 4 3 2 1